BRIEF TESTIMONY
OF
MY DEATH

BASED ON A REAL EVEN

Gerardo Sánchez

Copyright © 1996 Gerardo Sánchez
Breve Testimonio de mi Muerte
Translation by Zilia L. Laje
Reviewed by Nicole Sauceda

First edition 2010
www.gerardo-sanchez.net

ISBN 0-9652580-1-7
Catalog Card Number 98-093214
Congress Library USA

Being born and dying
are not two different states,
are different aspects
of one state.

Mahatma Gandhi

PROLOGUE

I was extremely impressed when Gerardo Sanchez told me, as a confession, the secret he had kept for many years, about his death. Some time later, he told me that he had decided to make his paranormal experience public.

In *"A Brief Testimony of my Death"*, the author describes, in a concise and entertaining narrative, without turning it into a novelistic work, how his death came about, his soul's separation from his body, the discovery of other worlds and other lives, as well as the retrospection of some of his past reincarnations and the amazing visions that-as prophecies-were reveal to him by an unknown power.

What surprised me the most was being able to subsequently confirm many of the facts present in Mr. Sanchez's narrative during the September eleven terrorist attacks in Washington DC and New York City. I understood then that those events as well as Osama Bin Laden's image were vividly shown to him twelve years, before they actually took place and when the author was dead.

This is a gripping testimony, where life and death are intertwined with the tragedies, misfortunes, joys of more than one existence. It shows us an endless and continuous cycle where life and death are not opposite things, but two different states of one and the same thing: the human existence.

BISHOP ORLANDO H. LIMA

INTRODUCTION

For five years I kept secret what I narrate in the contents of this text. During the first three, when I resided in Cuba, in a society where talking or even thinking about those subjects is absolutely forbidden, where everything related to spirituality is considered taboo, since the political system in essence denies the existence of everything spiritual and even the existence of God and as a consequence the majority of the population remains ignorant of all type of knowledge which is not supported in the precepts that praise a system based on pure dialectic materialism, somewhat confused, I first considered that my experience had been a dream or a nightmare, although I always had deep doubts about it. Inside I had, during that time, the persistent restlessness, the desire to know, to consult someone trustworthy about my experience, which I did not dare share with even my best and closest friend, for fear he would consider me crazy, a liar or fantasy-filled.

It was not until two years ago, in 1993, when I came to live in the United States, where I started to enjoy freedom of speech and action, when I started to get some information about everything related to the knowledge that a developed and free society has as far as subjects like the one I deal with in this testimony, that I understood how natural my experience was.

Consulting with a very good friend, a Cuban former minister of a Protestant church, to whom I told my experience, not in great detail, it was that I fully understood that everything that had happened to me could be normal and that it would be interesting, in his opinion, if it were written for the knowledge of others, since it is extremely rare that death, to so call it, could be known and narrated. For that reason I took to the task of compiling my notes and writing my memories to that respect, trying not to omit details and to express, with great difficulty I must say, what I had experienced, since it is tremendously difficult to explain in words what we "live" when we liberate ourselves from our physical bodies, since in "death" there is no communication in words and everything is based on a natural and perfect telepathic intercommunication.

In this text I have tried not to omit anything, as I previously expressed, and I have based myself strictly on what really happened, without adding any detail, in the simplest manner possible and with the greatest clarity that the written work allows, trying at every moment to transmit to the reader that this is not a supernatural event and that every human being is a part of one existence, that in what is material as in what is spiritual, we belong to a space of which we form an integral part in a natural process of physic-biological as well as energetic progress and evolution, which is simply no more than life itself.

We are part of a marvelous world in material and spiritual riches which we don't fully value and which we generally do not know or refuse to know, absorbed in giving priority to daily routines. Because of that ignorance, from which most of us human beings suffer, we find ourselves sunk in a world full of social differences, miscarried intents, half-way successes, doubts as to which road to take in life and frustrations; and we know ourselves as little as we know others, we underrate and undervalue ourselves and worst of all we do not know how to find the road of improvement to be or try to be what we should really be: the perfection of creation –because we *are* made and endowed for it,- enlarging the existing chasm between each other more all the time, which carries us to our physical and spiritual destruction, exterminating in our path everything beautiful that nature and man, as a part of it, have created.

Because of my experience, brief but rich in teaching, and because of everything in general that happens in the world, I now feel that the time in which mankind could take a turn, correct and amend great errors is almost reaching its end and it would be almost a miracle if we human being changed the course of our history full of abuses, devastating wars, vices, crimes and misunderstanding.

Only love can save us, only tolerance and our conciliation with ourselves and with others, establishing with conviction a perfect harmony between physical body and spirit, between conscience and true peace, would allow as to continue our eternal life once outside our body, in a better world of which we all, by nature, have a right to be a part.

The purpose of this text does not intend to educate the reader or influence him to base his life in another's experience, which he might consider supernatural and in part lacking credibility, but to make him meditate about himself and about the world around him and of which he is a part, all analysis remaining open as to the material and spiritual life, to so call it, each one from his own outlook, since there are no better analysts in this respect than ourselves if we concentrate on the task of valuing ourselves, making a recount of our walk through this life, and to meditate about everything positive or negative which resulted from our way of acting and speaking, and the way of projecting our feelings toward those who directly or indirectly are or were in contact with us. To meditate, not only about those results, but also about how much spiritual richness we have accumulated positively or negatively, and what we have offered in our path through life as to what is material and what is spiritual, which is the most important, and to what degree we have been capable of recognizing errors made and with how much honesty toward ourselves we have repented and amended ourselves.

I know that this testimony will cause you to meditate and discuss about this and many other.

THE AUTHOR

BRIEF TESTIMONY
OF
MY DEATH

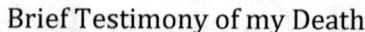

THE MATERIAL WORLD

It was the month of November 1989, when times were becoming mighty unbearable in the city of Havana, given the dire economic and sociopolitical situation faced by the nation, which promoted and increase in juvenile delinquency and danger in the streets of the city.

Few people dared leave their homes late at night, mainly in the old area of the city, where darkness prevailed in the narrow and deserted streets. In spite of everything, a few of us dared walk through them to visit a coffee shop or some night spot where, because of its privacy and colonial charm, one could enjoy very cozy moments, and friends would meet to have a cup of coffee or a glass of iced tea and to comment on the latest events.

On one such evening I was bored and felt confined at home, where I lived with my mother. I decided to go out and take a stroll through old Havana, where I felt so pleased and liked so much to walk down some of the same stretches covered so many times. I dressed in a hurry. I looked at my watch; it was ten o'clock.

When I was about to open the front door, my mother came up to me making a gesture, placing her hand on her chest. I knew what she was going to say, it was the same advice so often repeated.

-Son, don't go out tonight, it's too late to be in the street and I worry when you go out this late.

-Don't worry, nothing is going to happen and besides, I'm going to come home early and I'll even be with people, because I expect to meet some friends. -I answered her in a soothing tone.

When the door closed behind me, I felt a certain almost imperceptible inner uneasiness, like a hidden fear or an unexplainable strange misgiving, as flitting as a flash of light, which I attributed to the fact of knowing that my mother was left alone and a little worried about me. "It's normal in a mother", I said to myself.

When I had walked a block, I saw the bus nearing the stop and ran a few yards to catch it, I was the last one to board and stayed almost hanging from the door, since it was so full, that the crowd didn't let me get in. I travelled almost a mile that way. For an instant I thought of getting off and going back home, but I didn't do it.

After approximately 45 minutes, I arrived in Old Havana. I got off that infernal machine and started my usual walk through the nearly dark but very familiar streets, which took me to a known very old colonial building, "El Patio" restaurant, located facing the Plaza of the Cathedral and one block away from the latter. This was undoubtedly one of the most picturesque places in Old Havana. There I expected to meet with a few who usually, like me, attended several times a week.

I was walking east down Obispo Street in the direction of the Bay to reach San Ignacio Street and turn left. The evening was a little cold and few pedestrians walked at that hour around the city, especially down the street where I was. All along the stretch of street I must walk there were only three lights shining down from some lampposts located on the corners, several blocks ones from the others, the faint beam of light from each therefore fusing in a few yards into the dark of the night, and the scant dim lights that shone from some houses hardly lighted one or two yards of the sidewalk in front of them. There were moments when I had to look carefully where I walked because I could not distinguish clearly where I was stepping. There was an instant, on reaching a poorly lighted corner, when I stopped for a few seconds to check my watch. When I lifted my eyes to go on, I saw a couple of closely linked lovers some twenty yards from me who were walking enveloped by the darkness down the same sidewalk in the opposite direction. We passed, getting further away from the light at the same time and again entering the dark night. I suddenly thought I heard steps behind me and I turned to look, but didn't see anybody. At my back there was only a crumbled old big porch full of debris and rubbish from what had once been a beautiful house.

I was continuing my walk when suddenly two shadows pounced on me. I caught sight of two men with strong and muscular bodies and skin as dark as the night, because some light from the lamppost on the corner reached us. I tried to dodge them with a brusque movement to break into a run, but I could not, because I suddenly felt myself pressed against a column by those two forces much greater than me next to my body, restraining me.

-Grab him by the neck. I'll take his watch and chain-. One said to the other. So close was his face to mine that he sprayed me with saliva when he spoke.

When one of them tried to take my wrist to unfasten the wristwatch, he stopped pressing me against the column and I felt free from the pressure of both. I gave a strong tug and could get away from their grip ready to run, but could only get a few feet away.

PASSAGE TO THE INVISIBLE WORLD

A hard blow to the head shook my whole body so violently that I fell forward from the push. I extended my arms in front trying to hold on to something, which I did not find, and I tumbled to the sidewalk. I still remember clearly the nasty sensation I experienced feeling on my cheek the moist and gritty surface of the pavement and the stench that arose from it. Then I felt a blow on my brain like the tick of the clock.

It all happened in a fraction of a second. I immediately stood up with a swiftness that today seems inexplicable and I saw how two men ran away terrified and got lost in the dark on turning a corner. My helplessness and desperation had no limit. I yelled, "Help, help, I've been robed!", but nobody seemed to hear me. I turned on my heels and felt a great relief. The couple of lovers who had passed me a moment ago were rushing toward me and a dark-skinned, heavy lady of about fifty was also approaching with an expression at once of astonishment and pity.

The three were near me, about a yard away. They were so close together that their bodies almost brushed against each other.

-We have to call an ambulance. -Said the dark woman-. He looks dead.

-Yes we have to do something fast. – Agreed the young lady making up the couple.

Something confused me and astonished me. I was talking to those people and they did not seem interested in what I was saying to them! They were ignoring me completely. I wondered at their stupidity, that after being witnesses to what they had seen, they didn't even care how bad I felt and what my state of suffering was after having lived such a terrible experience. The more I talked and yelled in the midst of my nervousness, the more they ignored me, the more intense and excited their conversation turned amongst them. They did not look at me, they were concentrating their attention on the floor until I unconsciously looked down at the pavement at my feet.

There, near me on the sidewalk was the body of a man, lying face down, with his arms spread almost in a cross. A trickle of blood ran down his neck. I knew his figure, something in him was familiar, even his clothes seemed known. I felt a tremor inside. I couldn't believe what I was looking at!

-It cannot be! It cannot be! –I mumbled very softly.

It was I who was lying on the floor! Overwhelmed and confused, I separated from the group that didn't see me or hear me, crossed the street to the opposite side and leaned against the old wall of a house, distressed, while I saw some five yards away, on the other side of the street, how the group of onlookers was growing and they were adding up one by one. There were already about seven or eight persons surrounding the body.

It seemed impossible, that what I was seeing was a dream. "It was to be a nightmare from which I'll wake up at some point", I thought. Then I started remembering in detail everything that had happened a moment before and I realized that it did not look as if I were dead, as the dark woman had said on seeing the body lying on the sidewalk, but that... I *was* dead!

A mixture of desperation and surprise pervaded me. I felt agitated, I wanted to cry and the tears could not flow, I felt an enormous need to yell, to yell with all my strength, but it was useless, nobody could hear me.

-I'm dead... without a doubt. -I said with words that I did not hear and I lowered my head, crushed by the weight of the rough, surprising and striking reality.

A change started to take place in me. I felt as if I did not belong to that space of which I had been a part until seconds before. I no longer felt the cold of the night or enjoyed the pleasure so many times experienced when I looked at those places so loved and treasured in which a large part of my life had coursed, I didn't feel the breeze that came from the sea slide over my skin as I had a moment before, I didn't feel my clothes on my body, the smell disappeared from the air, but I discovered something new never before perceived. Was it life itself or maybe real death which had transformed me into part of all that was invisible to the world in which I had existed and which was at the same time another?, another dimension inside the same space, where I had the privilege of seeing and hearing all that went on around me.

While others did not have the slightest possibility of seeing beyond what the horizon of the landscape allowed them, or hear the softest and most imperceptible sounds, I enjoyed the gift of capturing all that was before me belonging to the material world and also what they could not see because they were not a part of the invisible world, the other dimension from which two times are appreciate in one space: the invisible world where I found myself by an unexpected turn of fate and the material world where I had existed. Now I was coldly, serenely and calmly looking at my own physical death.

I instantly stopped feeling the initial headache. The only thing left for me was waiting to see what would happen from that moment on.

As if moved by an inner strength, but which came from the universal energy, a force of natural knowledge which concentrated in my being and came from all directions and at the same time went every way, I started to think of myself, to observe and analyze what was really happening to me, what I really was at that moment. I noticed that my body was weightless and in order to move only the intention was needed. Only the least interest in taking a step was enough for me to move. I thought of standing again near the wall, from which I had unconsciously moved away while I looked around me and by only wishing it there I was again leaning against the cold and damp surface. Cold and damp that I could not feel due to the lack of physical body, but which I very clearly defined through a strange new sense impossible to explain. I then started to pay attention to a murmur that had reached me from the first few seconds, but to which, due to the first shock, I had not granted importance. I concentrated all my power of perception on that confusing sound that came from all directions. I started slowly scanning with my eyes all that surrounded me: the pavement of the street, the surface of the sidewalk, banisters, columns, walls, roofs, everything physical, trying to discover from where that mixture of confused and undefinable noises and murmurs originated. I sharpened my attention more. All my being captured like a receptor of energy the magnetic forces existing in space, it assimilated, processed and accumulated them to manufacture and conserve them, like the memory of a huge data processor. At each movement of my eyes by which I fixed my sight on any surface, a different and more defined sound came. I slowly traveled the length of sidewalk close to where I was. The sound of some footsteps came to my senses, I heard strong clatters of heels and slow steps, I could distinguish when the steps were those of the aged who dragged their feet with their tired walk, those of shushing men and women and an occasional run, even the trot of horses which made their hooves resound on the ground. The surface of the wall opposite, worn by the years, grayish and dirty from lack of paint and the accumulation of dust, kept echoes impregnated in its thick and compact mass. Voices reached me from it mixed with one another like a great din in different intensities: the crying of some babies, the yells of men with rough and strong voices, the calm and slow words of women in a dry and deep tone. They were not the voices of the few persons who were wandering the street, they were like energies arising from those stones and the cement, which surged from the whole block of stones and asphalt that the whole city formed. In each spot the energy and vitality had remained imprinted of every living being that lived or passed through those places, maybe some for a whole life and others from a short time perhaps. Nothing had been lost, vestiges of human and animal life with all its charge of vital energy had remained forever imprinted like a sign of life in the matter that surrounded them in the past. And I was there perceiving that miracle of creation, with the doors open to the truth of life in the fourth dimension and of which I was now a part!

Something was happening in that combination of murmurs and sounds that reached me, which escaped my understanding at that moment, since at the same time I listened, I perceived visually something indefinite in space, which confused me. It was the perception of the image, since although I very clearly identified the people who surrounded my body, I could see besides the outlines of human figures around in all types and shapes missed among them, which blended between the shadows and the lights with transparency and undefined strokes, who moved, appeared and disappeared like spirals of smoke in the open space. I could not find an explanation to what I was sensing. Was I a part of a fourth dimension very separate from the physical, or was there a middle point between the space and time I occupied and those occupied by the persons materially visible, which allowed me to capture two dimensions at the same time?

A great restlessness added itself to the initial striking moment. I thought of my mother, I remembered the times in which I hesitated whether to go on my trip on the bus or return home. I wondered doubtfully if that had been my fate or a coincidence to end my road in life. I felt afflicted by those thoughts. I was not prepared for such a brusque change.

A new transformation of feelings began in me, which I cannot determine in what fraction of a second started. The feelings gave way to another state –let's call it emotional,- in which I did not feel nervousness, fear, pain, happiness or sadness. A strange, healthy and sweet peace started to reign inside me.

THE DARKNESS
THE ASCENT

Only a furtive look upward which searched for an answer to everything so novel that had happened was enough to transform it all.

I raised my gaze to the starry sky and, as fast as lightning, everything changed. The stars disappeared from my sight, I looked down and everything turned completely dark. I was not being able to see anything else. I immediately experienced the sensation of being attracted upwards by an extraordinary force and I suddenly started to be absorbed from above as if a gigantic vacuum cleaner were sucking me in. An enormous and black vacuum surrounded me while I apparently rose, giving me the impression that I was traveling through an immense cave of infinite space through the central axis of which I moved upward in a straight line at a great speed.

What I experienced while my trip proceeded through that black and gloomy tunnel is the worst that I will remember forever. I didn't see anything but I knew I was not alone. Men's and women's voices started to reach me and others so strange that I could not define whether they were human or those of strange creatures, but they undoubtedly were voices. They did not have normal accents like those which we are used to hearing. They were cries of dread, wails, howls of horror and desperation as I had never heard before. I heard the fringing of teeth that gnashed perhaps repressing moans of pain, wails and despairing pleas.

I was accompanied by multitudes loudly crying for help, begging forgiveness. Heart-rending wails begging, pleading for relief. I didn't distinguish any figure clearly, but a natural recognition, like a telepathic transmission, made me understand everything painful and terrible that there was and was going on around me. For the first time I felt a terrible fear, uncontrollable, beyond all rational limits and terror seized me. When would that torture end? I asked myself. And my ascent continued.

I suddenly started to experience unknown feelings, very difficult to explain in words. All that world of wails, pain, panic and suffering that surrounded me, I started to understand, what would happen during the course of that experience and through that natural knowledge that is perceived in telepathic form from a higher force, was originated by remorse, the sense of guilt of those who wailed, as if they were indivisibly an integral part of that black space. It was as if their conducts, their conditions inside their kind, perhaps deformed or negative, prior to death had been, for a reason I do not know, the ones which led them and placed them in that situation, in that state. If hell exists, I think that was hell. I started to experience all the feelings of guilt, remorse, regret before a wrong done, as if I were one of those unfortunate beings condemned to remain in that empty space devoid of something good and pleasant. I suddenly looked up and high above, very far, distinguished a very intense light that turned from pale yellow to a shining white. But it was very far!

In the midst of that absolute darkness, in which I experienced the same feelings as those who desperately howled around me, I started to feel the whole scope of sensations caused in them by desperation and the agonizing frenzy of deep pain. And I became a part of all that.

A new view opened up before me not less unpleasant than the one formerly described. As if in a rewinding video, images started to appear of stages of my own past life and the memories, the feelings of my own guilt, of my own remorse seized me like daggers of fire, driving into my conscience and my memory, winding my innermost and most sensitive spiritual fibers. My conscience was being placed in check. My memories were being dug up and clarified so that there would not be any doubts and I would have full awareness as to why I was suffering what I was at that moment. I saw myself playing over scenes from my own life in which my behavior had not been good, pleasant or humane enough, leaving much to be desired, which was to cause pain, shame or suffering to other people, feeling which now rebounded toward me.

I was about fifteen and was in a classroom in the school I attended –that was the scene-. In a corner of the room as usual, was sitting a black boy everybody scorned, mistreated and used as the butt of all kinds of jokes, abuses that sometimes went beyond the verbal to the physical. I was standing in front of him. I was cruelly making offensive fun of him, I approached him and threatened him with gestures and as I neared him, he shrank in his seat as if he wanted to vanish into thin air. I did not take into account, was not conscious, that this game caused great pain in the heart of the defenseless, skinny and fearful boy, who did not dare raise his eyes for the terror that had accumulated in him after repeatedly suffering the abuse of all his classmates.

Seeing myself in that depressing scene, I felt ashamed, guilty, sad, depressed. I felt a desire to cry, to mend my behavior and would have done anything at that moment and now, to be again before the young boy, to kneel in front of him, beg forgiveness a thousand times and kiss his feet if it were necessary. What feeling of shame, guilt, remorse and loathing of myself I harbored in that instant! At the same time all the feeling of fear, desperation and impotence throbbed in me which the boy felt before so much mistreatment and display of unmercifulness. I wished to cry, but I did not have tears and the inability to do it increased my desperation.

I did not want to look at my past, but the view of this was there, showing me the scenes as if spitting on my face everything shameful and reprobate that my behavior inflicted. I now fully understand that only that type of feeling is experienced in the midst of that gloomy and completely dark tunnel. There is no room in there for anything noble or pleasant.

The Chinamen Manuel appeared, that little old man who sold greens and tubers at the corner shop. It was one of the occasions when I passed in front of his business and together with other young men made fun and yelled cruelties and ironic phrases.

Manuel sold his vegetables in a small shop, where the floor was always dirty, as were his clothes, due to the dirt that shed from the tubers. One could not distinguish where the fabric of his clothes ended over his body and where his skin started colored by the dirt. When he walked past a person, the smell of onion, garlic and others mixed with his sweat, made anybody turn his back waiting for Manuel to move away. He was respectful, pleasant and kind. That was the object of our mockery. Poor Manuel! His only "sin" was being very poor and working very hard to send all his savings to his family, left behind many years before in his native land. He lived in the midst of his vegetables, his memories and his loneliness, and perhaps his sorrows. I did not appreciate that, I only noticed the grime on his clothes, his dirty skin, how funny I found his strange way of walking, but I did not see everything clean and beautiful that was inside the little old Chinaman, who never complained about our scoffing and did not even bestow a glance on us, or a word of reproach or anger.

As I watched those scenes of my life, something twisted inside of me, a terrible remorse, shame and an incalculable, undescribable pain corroded me inside. What I would have given to hug Manuel the Chinaman at that moment, even today! If the circumstances had repeated themselves, with pleasure and satisfaction I would have cleaned his shop, washed his cloths or gotten him better ones, I would have tried to enrich his life, I would have hugged him with much love and respect. I ask myself, "Will there be a remedy and time for the remorse? Will there be a form to compensate all the wrong done in our lives? Will it be possible to avoid all that torture and agony that we will possibly one day experience in the black and infernal tunnel? Will that nightmare be temporary or eternal?"

The elderly lady Nena, a little Spanish woman who lived alone near my home, -it was another scene- was at her window. We gathered on her porch as if it were our own terrain, a group of young men, not respecting her property. She yelled at us many times from that very window not to annoy her with our fuss and noises just at the time of her nap. We dirtied her porch and didn't let her rest. That was our place of amusement almost every day to play cards, dominoes and so on, bothering and interrupting the elderly lady's rest, without heeding her justified words of complaint. She even cried on several occasions due to the nervousness and impotence at being unable to stop so much annoyance caused by us, who ignored her. She did not have relatives or anybody who would come out in her defense in any situation. I accused myself of cruelty on seeing that and I reproach myself now. I hated myself and regretted witnessing the scene not having received a good lesson or punishment for my wrongdoing I regret it today.

Event after event, one following the other in order, as they took place, were presenting themselves before my eyes. I experiences all the suffering the anguish and all the mixture of feelings that the victims suffered and all the feeling of regret and remorse of the victimizer. None of the moments in my life that repeated themselves were those in which I acted correctly or humanely, on good faith or with kindness. It seemed that the results from these would be the consequence of something that I did not know and which I would perhaps not be able to see or appreciate at that moment enveloped in the darkness.

As all this was happening something in me was renewing itself. I was obtaining conscience, which I still maintain, that the behavior that we held in our third dimension would result in the state in which we would proceed to the other life. That is, that the result of the purification of our spirit, of the cleanliness of feelings and actions, of our capacity to understand the realities of others and the respect of the behavior, wishes and acts of the others, the respect of their tastes, preferences and rights, will be the thermometer or the yardstick with which our merits will be measured for the other stages of our life. I understood that since we are born until we die we must be lenient with others and with ourselves, learn at each instant all that is shown to our eyes and ears by natural law, that nothing is supernatural and irrational and that everything has a reason, that everything is justifiable except bad behavior, no matter what type it may be or in which manner it may project itself, even when we act unconsciously. That the learning does not end with the physical death, but that one continues obtaining knowledge for all eternity as a spiritual being.

While I continued perceiving these views on my life, I did not stop hearing the wails and the tremendous frenzy that encompassed all the infinite black space. Very near me arms extended in my direction, tried to reach me desperately as if I were the anchor of salvation that, ascending, would take them out of that macabre deep miry place. They knew of my presence, recognized my transit among them. Although I knew of their extreme efforts to reach me, another unknown force, another hidden company of great power that did not manifest itself to me kept a certain distance or limit between my being and the others, creating an insurmountable barrier that prevented any direct interrelation. During the whole trip through the black tunnel, the feeling of ascent did not stop even for an instant. My course toward the heights continued with indescribable speed.

THE LIGHT

A tremendously bright light of immeasurable size shone high above. Little by little it grew and placed itself closer. Its presence, as if by a spell, diminished all the desperation and anguish which seized me in the midst of the total surrounding shadow.

The predominant color of the light in that enormous flashing mass was a very pale yellow, almost white. As this extended toward the edges, it turned orange, but it never completely defined itself exactly in that color. All that mass issued flashes of light like lightning in a straight line in every direction which shone with blinding reflexes. On its edges the flashes turned longer, giving the impression of an aurora borealis being integrated. The last rays of light from its borders continuously varied in size and intensity, each in different iridescent shades, all the colors of the rainbow in disorderly fashion becoming a part of them, with a marvelously harmonious and throbbing rhythm. The whole enormous ball of light presented a beating of colors and shades with glows that attracted, like a magnet, everything positive and beautiful that could exist in the infinite space of the universe.

As the light concentrated in its middle, it turned lighter and brighter. This seemed an enormous diamond of thousands of karats the faces of which issued beams of a very bright light flashing rays of a white that almost touched on silver. So intense and resplendent was this luminous center that it was impossible to watch steadily. The central point of this luminosity looked like a cloud of mixed smoke and water which undulated with rhythmic pulsations as if the whole gestating power of life in all its manifestations were concentrated in it.

As I neared that light I felt as if I were becoming a part of it. I foreboded or imagined what I was going to witness. I did not know what exactly it could be, it was like a premonition of the reencounter with that unknown memory of which was at the same time filed in my subconscious. It was like returning to the starting point without remembering which that point was or what it was like.

The light continued growing before me, but I did not perceive it from beneath any longer but in front, since I had in my transit spun inside that ascending spiral and was left floating in space, standing upright in front of it.

THE FIRST ENCOUNTER

I cannot imagine or even approximately calculate at what distance I was from that light. I had already gotten close enough to suppose that I was about be touched by one of its beams. An enormous wall that was in front of me extended upward, down and to both sides with an infinite glow. I continued advancing towards the central point which was turning more brilliant, moved by a very superior power, which kept transmitting to me in a natural way all the knowledge, findings and understanding of everything that I witnessed and which became engraved in my mind forever.

The area, cloudy and wavy like a sea, central to that point, became gradually larger and from its whiteness violet shades could be seen very pale and sparkling like powdered diamonds. That swell got closer and closer, to such an extent that I thought for an instant that it would fall on me. One last wave of the nebulous light became larger than the others and like a tidal wave rushing in my direction it overturned on me. I felt an inexplicable violent charge of energy and vigor in my being; however, the ecstasy in which I was submerged did not allow me to feel any stimulating impression which would alter me. Totally absent from me from that moment on were fear, nervousness, pain, bad memories, happiness or sadness. A total peace seized me from the innermost fibers of my being. That peace gushed from me and fused with a similar one coming from the light, as if were all the same time in an intimate interrelation formed a part of a general common calm.

My course stopped for an instant. It was the first moment in which I felt steady, without floating; it was the moment in which the force of absorption stopped.

Suddenly, the frame of a large doorway was appeared before me. Mi visual perception was concentrating on the center point exactly in front of me when this door opened, not as a door normally supposed opens, but a rectangle drew away from that wall of light vanishing in space like smoke and the doorway stood accessible to allow passage.

The feeling of peace increased in me, an undescribable serenity which I had never experienced or have never repeated in my life. A state of sweet tenderness and joy filled my being, a feeling of absolute rest.

That entire luminous and confused image became gradually more real and the details before my eyes were slowly defined. The outside clarity that I first saw slowly disappeared and all the intense light now came from inside the enormous space on the other side of the opening. Next to the large frame the first human figure appeared in my new dimension I perceived clearly with serenity and confidence. It was the figure of a woman known to me. I passed the threshold and stopped next to it, very near that human figure. It was a woman advanced in age, she wore a simple white dress, slippers of the same color and her long hair, straight and very gray, was plaited in a braid placed on the nape of her neck in the form of a bun. Two combs held her hair at either side of her head. Her skirt reached down to her ankles. She was short, and her passed barely my shoulders. My mother had, in her stories about the family, talked to me many times about that little old lady with a wrinkled face weathered by the sun and the harsh toil of a whole lifetime in farm chores, whom I knew only through and old photograph which the family kept as cherished memories and once or twice I looked at without taking much interest. She was my mother's grandmother, who had died before I was born. What happiness, what tenderness I felt on beholding her image! Her calm and sweet face inspired love and tranquility. Her tender and very loving gaze rested on me like a blessing.

The first instant having passed and the first impression claimed, a whole slew of questions rushed to my mind and as if by a supreme spell her voice reached me. There were no words, neither were any necessary. A perfect telepathic communication richer and more complete in transmission of concepts than the spoken word, a natural knowledge interrelated between the two sufficed which fused with the wise energy accumulated in the space we shared and allowed us to understand each other with a simple, clear and perfect communication.

-Son, -she said with a soft and murmuring voice which exceeded the limits of tenderness and gladness- I am glad you are with me. I knew you were coming. I expected you. I am surprised, because this is not your time or your moment to come to us, since your mission is not accomplished. You have to go back.

She approached me with soft and slow steps while she said these words. Her arms reached out to me and we embraced. That energetic and sublime contact charged with tenderness transmitted an uncomparable and unexplicable feeling of sweetness and peace to me.

-What place is this? –I asked- Why am I here? What beautiful place is this?

She drew apart from me when she perceived my words. A white and subtle light surrounded her body. A halo of light edged her whole figure and the aura glowed on her head with a more intense luminosity. As she talked to me, her own light intensified its glow with soft blue and silver shades announcing that woman's passion at meeting me.

-I feel very well here, -I went on saying. -Why do I have to return?

I felt in such a perfect spiritual state that I refused to accept the idea of having to leave. A fast thought raced through my mind. I wanted to see, I wanted to know that resplendent world. She, interpreting my wish, held her hand out to me and took mine wordlessly.

-I am going to show you only what you may and should see. You will have to return later because your moment has not yet come-, she said again.

Knowing of her presence at my side, feeling the contact of her energy through my hand, I stopped looking at her and directed all my attention to what was, as if by magic, starting to appear before my eyes. I saw the most beautiful, perfect and fascinating view that any human being may ever seen or imagine. If it was a dream, I did not want to wake up!

LIFE IN THE WORLD OF LIGHT

A marvelous natural landscape extended before me. I did not observe constructions or structures there, nature prevailed in all its splendor. The surface or plane on which I found myself standing extended in a straight line giving the impression that it was a flat world and not round, as in our physical life, which made the horizon appear further, tremendously far. There was no sun; however, a very white light pervaded all the open space. In that world it was always daylight.

In the forefront, a plain extended with slight hills and valleys, colored with a very pale soft emerald green in which oasis of reverberating and leafy vegetation appeared at intervals. Further away, to my right, were trees around which ferns and plants of elegant and svelte structure in a great variety were clustered and lakes of peaceful waters a little further away looked like a mirror in which everything that surrounded it were reflected, beautiful trees alternated with the plentiful vegetation of its shores. To my left the landscape presented a composition of hills of low and medium height punctuated in the distance by taller elevations the tops of which gleamed with a very pale green color, almost white. In the whole landscape, where the grass was very short, I saw medium-size stones which came about halfway up my legs, smooth and positioned so that they seemed placed by a gardener of exquisite artistic taste. I did not see dry leaves on the fields nor withered lawns, fallen or dry trunks anywhere. Everything seemed to be in the plenitude of its splendor and life.

Clusters of plants appeared very harmoniously distributed throughout the landscape with the most diverse and beautiful flowers in thousands of different colors and soft hues. None had an intensely pure color, giving the impression that they were softened with the shade that prevailed over everything visible.

No color existed in that entire beautiful world which prevailed in its pure shade. Every shade was low. Not even the most genial painter could have portrayed the magnificence of such beautiful and perfect nature.

Enriching that entire infinite garden was the presence of animals of every type. Birds of beautiful feathers and varied colors were perched on the branches of the tall trees and some flew at medium altitude with their beautiful wings spread as if a soft wind took care of carrying them through space. Four-legged animals of great variety walked among the flowers and some stood on the edge of the ponds that reflected their shape, on the peaceful waters of which rested lotuses of beautiful colors and great variety. In the background beautiful cascades of clear water came down which splashed over the rocks decorated by the white fronts of the breaker. Nothing altered the peace of the place.

Everything within my view, plants, water, stones, animals, and even the very space glowed with its own light. The light was there, no star was needed to light all that beauty. Whatever existed in that fascinating and attractive world issued luminous reflections and haloes of soft glowing whiteness edged everything the leaves of the plants, the flowers, the stones and the animals, as if a vital powerful energy concentrated in each being, in each thing. It seemed that even the stones had life.

Far away, where the landscape lost itself the distant skyline, the sky glowed as if in an orange sunset, like a variegated aurora borealis from the shade of almost reddish orange to the purest white that, as it grew closer, turned into a very pale emerald color, then into violet until it transformed into the blue that prevailed in the sky, a sky in which there was no sun. A sky that, being lit, allowed seeing twinkling little and very luminous sparks in it like those of the stars in the night. The whole of celestial preciousness was completed by some very white clouds like cotton balls which splattered the blue space.

The immense reigning quiet, in the plane on which I stepped as well as in space, produced in me an ecstasy and a peace that made me feel a part of all that, as if everything were a single essence, a unity in which the internal and external harmonies joined perfectly.

INHABITANTS OF THE LIGHT

So ecstatic was I watching the sublime and marvelous place where I found myself, trying to get further and further into that magnificent nature of alluring image and contagious quiet, that I did not realize that I was no longer alone. Besides the little old lady, who did not leave my side, some persons had started coming close proceeding from different directions. Other were far as if they were not aware of my presence. They were the inhabitants of that paradise who had blended into the landscape creating the composition of the perfect image of life, perhaps never imagined by anybody.

No state of mind altered my being in spite of all that I was seeing, no feeling of grief, preoccupation, restlessness, happiness or sadness, even after so rude a change as the one suffered in my existence, captivated by the environment that surrounded me where no cold or heat was felt. I divined the pleasant warm aroma which pervaded the surrounding space. There were no perceptible noises that total silence being the culminating complement of that harmonious and permanent peace.

Men and women of different ages surrounded me. Most of the closer ones were elderly, unknown to me, but who transmitted to me the confidence that is felt when we are before persons very familiar, trusted and loved. I was pleasantly impressed by the physical and psychological appearance of those persons so special to me that I can still remember when I think of my experience. Especially that of an elderly man who was closer to me, with a deep and calm gaze. They all wore long tunics that reached down to their feet which remind me of the ancient Greeks, white, with sleeves down to their wrists and closed necklines in the Oriental custom. Some wore them in a violet color, others pink or very pale yellow. The necklines and sleeves, as well as the lower borders which brushed their feet were trimmed in the finest lace that seemed manufactured of the highest carat gold with inlays of diamonds, emeralds and sapphires which radiated marvelous flashes. Their waists were tied with beautiful belts that seemed made from the same material, but more beautiful and more loaded with stones and artistic beauty. These belts were knotted almost to one side and their long ends dropped heavily down past the knees of those who wore them. They were all dressed in the same style, an impressing style which inspired admiration and respect when joined with the sober and serene countenance of the persons who wore them. The men went bare-headed and they showed beautiful, white manes, others gray and some blond like gold which came down past their shoulders, and they wore a ribbon placed around their foreheads of a material identical to that with the belts seemed to have been manufactured. The women, dressed the same as the men, covered their heads with long kerchiefs which reached almost down to their waists.

Slow but eloquent gestures and manners gradually gave me access to participate in that circle of persons. They had been there for a very long time, a time which I could not calculate, but which was immense. And as if giving an answer to my unrest, in an instant other familiar faces started appearing among them. Very familiar human faces those years before had shared my former existence and the daily living in the course of the material life. Persons who had died!

Felipe! Felipe was there! I couldn't believe it. He had been one of the persons I knew who had made me feel the most shocking and hard moments of anguish and desperations in my life when I was younger at a time I must have been about twenty. He was there before me, tangible, almost touchable, with his calm smile and that characteristic greeting of his consisted of a little wink of his left eye. That was his greeting after nineteen years, the same gesture he used in our last farewell years before, when neither one of us even remotely imagined that we would never again meet in the material world. He was there! Nothing had changed in his robust figure, nimble of movement and fast walk. It seemed time had not passed for him. He, as did all those present, had his own light, the glow of his body and his clothes was not less than that of the other people's and, as the others, as everything that existed in that world, around his head shone the halo of light, the aura.

We did not have to intend to take even a single step. In an instant we were joined in the most impassioned, sincere and fraternal embrace. It seemed impossible to me! And amid my happiness for the reunion, a sudden flash of nostalgia seized me. The memory crossed my mind like lightning of all our time of friendship, that short time in which I learned all about his sorrows and suffering.

I met Felipe on 1970. We were the same age. We were both fulfilling the b of the Mandatory Military Service in the Armed Forces in our respective military units. As fate would have it we landed in the same place, the military prison of Morro Castle, located on the east side of the entrance of the Havana Bay. I was sent there because I had deserted and was sentenced to an eighteen months' term. He faced a larges charge another person. He had escaped from his military unit in the night hours, but the other fired at the post and killed him. Felipe was charged with murder and was awaiting trail.

We were always in different galleys. I had the privilege of working all day away from my cell, but he was not granted that opportunity, given the situation and the reason why he was in jail. I met him in an occasion in which he called me when I passed before his cells, asking me to get him a little water and a piece of bread, because he was going very hungry. From that moment on, several times a day, behind the guard's backs, I sat before the bars of his cell to talk. Little by little we become friends and he gradually told me his tragedy and he also told me, among other things, that one of his great worries was not knowing about his mother, who had gone mad at his imprisonment and had been committed to an insane asylum.

I always believed in his innocence because the inmates used to confide the truth to each other with honesty, rawness and devoid of all taboo or prejudice, with no reservations. He assured me that he had never shot at anybody and I was sure of it.

Our friendship lasted almost a year, in which time I gradually develop a great love for him. I worried what the outcome would be the day of his trial, because all the indications and appearances, up to what I knew, pointed to his being found guilty, even though deep down I harbored the hope that justice and truth would prevail.

-The public prosecutor asks for the death penalty for me, - he told me anxiously on more than one occasion- and I am very afraid.

Many times he cried next to me, his hands tightening around the bars of his cell.

One day I was transferred to do some work in the office-fileroom of the attorney-general's office downtown and we separated without having the opportunity to let him know or say good bye. I do not remember on what occasion a military messenger, who was friendly with me and knew him, delivered a note to me from Felipe where he told me it was urgent for him to see me soon, that he had something very important to tell me, he was desperate. But I could not see him or contact him. I did not hear anything from him again until one day a document reached my hands by chance at the fileroom of the attorney-general's office. It was Felipe's signed death sentence, which had already been carried out. From that day on regret did not leave me in peace because I thought that, if I had gone to see him when he asked me to, maybe it would have done some good to cooperate with him in his favor and maybe he would not have been executed. It was more painful when six months later my certainty was confirmed. The true guilty party was found and also executed. My innocent and dear friend had died without guilt.

When we separated and the enchantment of that embrace was broken, I received his consolation. He did not reproach me of anything, he accepted his fate with calm and he demonstrated to me his happiness to be next to me at that instant and his full peace in his new and eternal existence, full of quiet and beauty, devoid of all the anguish and the pain that I had found in him when we first met. I assimilated his consolation; I perceived his love and infinite happiness. It seemed as if I needed that reencounter to erase my pain and so that my remorse would disappear for good. I was immensely happy to be able to share and verify his luck, and to be there together. He was still my eternal friend, he remembered me and loved me in spite of having lived for years in two different worlds and the memory would last forever as would the value of the friendship, the most beautiful gift that mortals enjoy. All his pain, desperation and grief, all his torture had been left behind and were well compensated with the happiness and the peace of that place.

He separated and when he moved away I felt that did not mean a definite farewell, that it was a "so long". It was my wish and still is that we be together again, but I did not know when or how long I would have to wait for this to happen, although I wished with all the strength of my soul to stay there forever.

On my right the silhouette of a woman approached me. I was amazed and at the same time pleased when I recognized. It was Andrea!, the neighbor who lived next door to me since my childhood and had seen me grow up. Many said sarcastically that she had ensured going straight to hell. Andre put up more than anybody with my misbehavior. Every year she took it upon herself to celebrate my birthday as a gift and proof of love. The woman whom I had always loved as my own family and had died five years before.

Since she was a child, as people who had always known her told me and according to her own words, she had been dedicated to prostitution in times when life was very difficult. People scorned her as a strange bug for her past. No woman wanted to be her friend, nobody accepted even her acquaintance, except for a very few understanding persons. They denied her a greeting and turned their backs on her when she walked near others in public. She represented the worst for everybody and provoked the feeling of scorn in many people. But nobody knew Andrea's feeling as I did. In spite of her mundane life and the little value that she placed on herself, her behavior was due to the needs that she suffered since she was a child and the wish to furnish clothes and food to her orphaned nephews and nieces and a sick sister. The feeling of compassion that she showed toward the needy was very significant and she did not spare giving what were necessary to another with a little happiness. She loved children, perhaps because she never had any. I received her love from very near. That homely, thin and stooped woman who arose revulsion in many always inspired the opposite in me. When I was sad and blue, I always received from her a word of soothing support, understanding, a loving pat. For that reason I missed her a lot when she died.

There was Andrea, next to me, with her ample smile, showing me all her teeth. I could feel her hand on my shoulder with sweet warmth. I felt extreme happiness seeing her again. She, the dirtiest one before everyone's eyes, the most scorned, the most reviled, the "dirty" one shone more than anyone there. She showed her cleanliness. How many recollections from my childhood and youth, almost erased by the years, returned to my memory in her presence! How many moments of bustle, merriment and happy din

I remembered experiencing when we lived as neighbors! I feel like laughing when I remember those off-color jokes that she brazenly told in front of me and which transmitted so much mischief and wickedness. In her presence I received the teaching; not a thing matters in order to enjoy the privilege of living in the marvelous peace of that place, others than the purity of feeling and love that we may lodge and profess in life and everything good that we may be capable to offering our neighbor, even though we may not know how to give ourselves our own material worth, the worth that men have invented to justify their faults and establish differences.

She parted from me, always smiling, as if mischievously saying to me, "I'll be waiting for you here!"

The reunions continued, now without much communication. I only experienced joy and soothing gladness and peace which they wisely transmitted and which were a necessary and useful balm for me, for my soul in my present and in the future. Relatives of mine deceased years before, my grandparents, uncles, fiends paraded before me with the same peace, the same glow issuing from their figures and with those haloes of light that surrounded their heads and their bodies, and an occasional familiar face which, one way or another, meant something in my life at some point, some that I had already forgotten, but who still remembered me, as if the universal memory existing there had made my existence pulsate from the other dimension and in the memory of everyone and of all that universe of intelligence.

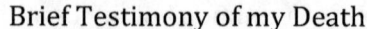

A PARADISE – STRANGE BEINGS

While I observed and enjoyed that miracle or creation, all my senses of perception concentrating on the magnificence displayed before me, I felt needed and anxious to be definitely a part of that world, and I think with joy and satisfaction of the happiness and good fortune that I had in reaching that place. A secret eagerness urged me to see more, to learn what there was of divine in that world where everything was in conformity, in which harmony had reached its maximum perfection and there were no differences, where one person's law did not prevail or that of a group, but the universal law of innate and natural intelligence which maintained an undoubtedly unbreakable and unalterable discipline in harmony and order.

On observing each plant, each leaf, each flower, the beautiful birds, the rocks, everyone and everything that my sight covered, I asked myself feeling that I imagined the answer, the manner in which that vital energy that was in each being in each thing had arrived at that dimension, that plane. It seemed as if each stone, each vegetable, each animal, each person had transferred with more beauty, more splendor and better forms to that plane, crossing the barriers of mortality. The most insignificant "living" being had importance in that place. Everything had value; everything had a spark of its own light, of life.

-Am I really dead or is this a dream? -I wondered.

The elderly man who was near me looked at me again with that look that I will never be able to forget, calm, deep, intelligent, wise. I felt his soft voice of clear, low and rich vibrating tone inside me.

-You are not dead, because death does not exist.

How to understand that new concept? How to be able to define true life or true death? At what point in our existence does life start or does death? My anxiety to know more grew with an imperative force from the innermost depth of my being. He knew it, they all knew it, they all knew what was on my mind, in my astral inside.

The elderly man looked at the elderly lady who had once been my family. I immediately interpreted his gesture. The moment had arrived to end that extraordinary meeting. I wanted to express something, but everything inside me was blocked, as if an external intelligent force controlled my transit on that plane. I felt sad for the first time, because I really did not accept, as I have never accepted, the return.

-Son, -said the elderly lady-, you may not stay here any longer. Your moment has not arrived. This is not the time. Let's go. And, always holding hands, she led me to the doorway through which I entered before. The elderly man followed us close. I looked back with the hidden hope my gaze would meet with one of those whom I loved so much, but they all had turned their backs on me and were moving slowly away without showing some effect that my presence there might have caused on them, except for the elderly man who was always close to me. His voice reached me again.

-What I am going to show you on your return is important-, he said.

What else could the sweet man show me, more novel, impressing or divine than everything I had seen? However, given the plenitude of knowledge and the perfect interrelation and interchange through natural communication which so easily flowed telepathically, it was not to be that he, as all, including my great-grandmother, perfectly interpreted my ambition to know more than I had seen, of all that I imagined could be possible on that plane and which I could not fully know during my stay there for reasons I cannot imagine.

While I headed toward the doorway led by the sweet little old lady and followed by the elderly man, nothing new happened. I knew that everything there had come to an end for me. Today I harbor the intimate hope that luck and my fate may someday as soon as possible lead me definitely back to that marvelous place from which I would have never wanted to return.

A last look around me and something very strange happened. To my right at a distance, appeared, or perhaps it had always been there and I had not been aware of its presence, a group of approximately six beings very different from humans, although in general they had certain similarities to us. They were beings of very low height, extremely thin, dressed in the custom of all the others as I formerly described, but with shorter garments. Their very thin arms and legs greatly caught my attention when comparing their heads disproportionally large with respect to the rest of their body. Their ears were big and slightly pointy at their upper and lower ends, which gave them a certain diabolic appearance. Their bulging eyes set at a slanted angle and with very small pupils looked at me with an expression of grandiloquence. Their faces showed a strange overacted way of laughing, their skin wrinkling all around their eyes and on their whole cheeks. Their skin was a strange greenish yellow color. As paper dolls they all raised both their arms pointing at me with their fingers at once which I interpret as a strange sign of farewell. I did not see anything more.

A bluish light suddenly enveloped me mixed with a strange fog which spun around me like a whirlwind and it all disappeared. I totally stopped perceiving.

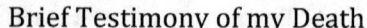

MY INCARNATIONS

I again saw myself surrounded by a different view and various scenes which succeeded one another in a very different boundary from that previously seen. They did not appear as suddenly as had happened a moment before. These were gradually taking shape at the same time the cloudy mass that enveloped me was dispelling, and they were defining themselves like the images in the memory of an old dream.

This time a known world and a natural life rose around me. An existence new and so novel that it initially confused me. I felt lost. I found myself surrounded by old and gray walls of high measurements. In the initial instant I could not exactly define what I perceived as I observed wondering. Little by little, as someone coming back to reality, I could start appreciating everything that surrounded me.

I found myself in the middle of an ample room. The walls were built with enormous stone blocks perfectly cut rectangularly. A fine black thread clearly drew their joint making the contrast with their gray color stand out. A large single-leaf door to my right remained wide open. Huge nails placed a short distance from each other in diagonal rows and all around the border trimmed the thick and dark woods of which it was made.

At the other end of the large rectangular room another similar door remained closed. I was standing almost in the middle of the room leaning on the back of a huge, sturdy, massive and dark wooden armchair, with deep carvings in its structure. I was looking out through an enormous window which allowed me to watch an arid landscape poor in vegetation in which not a single tree grew. It was an immense plain through which narrow dusty paths snaked under the burning sun.

Furniture did not abound in the room and large empty expanses allowed walking freely around it. Three seats similar to the one on which I was leaning were arranged in a circle. Shining armors of a glimmering silver in each corner remained stationary and standing like pieces in a antique museum. Higher than the windows, on the wall that was before me, almost from the ceiling hung an enormous red tapestry with heraldic emblems embroidered in yellow gold.

A huge, bulky and obviously very heavy black iron lamp hung from the middle of the ceiling reaching down to a few feet over my head. Unlit big and think ocher colored candles were placed on its multiple arched arms.

In the midst of the environment that surrounded me I did not hear voices and no exchange of knowledge or ideas existed, as happened in the plane of light. Everything was noiseless as in the silent film pictures, where only the gestures and movements transmitted the message and were the only means of understanding. The scenes displayed themselves before me in the same manner. Besides I was alone at that moment and could not perceive any communication from another person.

I started walking toward the closed door. Once before it, I started slowly to open it and at that instant I started to experience an acute depression, a great exhaustion and a deep gloom, proofs of a great emotional affliction. I felt a strong urge to cry and my chest was oppressing itself pervaded by a deep sorrow, a profound pain. A horrible suffering moved me from my innermost being.

The large door open, I went into a large room furnished in the same style as the previous room. It was a bedroom. By way of furniture there was only a large bed with tall posters of lathed wood in each corner, a huge table sat against a side wall, a large mirror and under this a table that apparently served as a dressing one. There were no windows in the room and the only lighting there was at that moment was the natural light that came in through the door I had just opened.

I headed for a small stand set next to the head of the bed. There was a bronze metal pitcher on it full of water, next to it a container apparently made of the same material, covered with a lid. I felt I was going to faint, that the suffering tore me to such an extent as if I were going to collapse at any moment. I wanted to put an end to it all. I placed one hand on the little stand to stay on my feet, while with the other one I poured a white powder into the water from a small bottle that was on the little stand. I drank the water slowly walked before the mirror and I saw myself. It was not my image which was reflected in the mirror! I felt perplexity and confusion which mixed with the deep suffering I was experiencing, creating a strange indefinable state of mind. In the mirror was reflected the figure of a woman, a beautiful woman with very fair skin, gold color hair and very blue eyes with a profound and serene gaze disturbed by a grimace of pain. Her hair was pulled straight back on either side and gathered at the back with a showy clasp from which fell a long curly mane. Her hands were slender and beautiful; she wore a ring on each with a white gem. The blue colored gown of a fabric similar to velvet, long sleeves down to her wrists and the full skirt almost trailing on the floor bestowed elegance and majestic personality on her figure.

I started to see myself in that woman. I broke out in sobs and gave free rein to the release of a deep pain. With my head leaning on my chest I gave vent to all my pain. I suddenly started to feel a strong ache in my stomach spread to the whole trunk of my body, I twisted from the physical pain, a horrible pain that seemed like daggers piercing my entrails. I fell on my knees. I tried to support myself grasping the edge of the stand with my hands, but I did not have the strength and I collapsed to the floor.

I straightened up moved by the expectation and the scare and I saw myself separated from the mirror which had reflected my other image. Now I was at a distance from which I could behold the whole view. I watched the beautiful lady who when falling dragged down some articles, which had apparently made a lot of noise and attracted the attention of others. The silent scene continued developing before me.

A man wearing a breastplate similar to the ones I had seen in the next room rushed into the bedroom and, although I did not hear anything or perceive the slightest noise, I realized perfectly well that he yelled giving the voice of alarm. Immediately another thin woman with very fair skin, tall, very humbly dressed all in black, who due to her appearance I suppose was a servant, came in hurriedly and fell to her knees next to the dead lady, crying while she took her hands in her own.

I immediately became convinced that I had lived in that woman's body, that in a very distant past I was embodied in it, in a beautiful and elegant lady who obviously belonged to the high class of those times.

From the landscapes, the type of construction where I was, the styles of clothes and furniture, I consider that those events took place during the Middle Ages and the scenes I lived happened in a castle of the period, very insulated from other populated places.

I had witnessed and experienced my death in an incarnation. "How old am I really? Can it be possible that a being may live more than one life or multiple ones?" I think that unknown is somewhat difficult to explain.

I was again enveloped by the haze that took me there, but on this occasion I sensed a companion, I felt the security of a presence next to me, which I cannot define and about which I do not have the slightest idea. It was the same feeling of company that I experienced during my ascent through the black tunnel in the first moments. This companion transmitted a sense of security, confidence, protection that was the permanent tranquilizer that controlled my excited instants and the agitated moments I was living.

As if by magic, the fog drew aside its curtain and gave way to a new reincarnation experience. I have no doubt that through a strange design, maybe by the condescension of a superior Something to my unrest and anxiety to see and know more, or perhaps by a supreme Will, I had the opportunity of seeing my deaths in different lives of the third dimension from that plane, in a retrospective view.

The sun was burning and it scalded my back. The great humidity of the environment made the sun felt more intensely. I desperately ran through the underbrush, I felt my legs could no longer endure. The exuberant vegetation closed my path. At intervals when I went out in the open field, it seemed more than run I flew over the pastures, but when I went further into the jungle it was much harder for me to make way in spite of finding myself in my medium. My body was covered with scratches caused by the fast brushing of the thicket against my skin and some wounds bled quite a lot, leaving behind a trail of red stains on the vegetation.

I was alone, on the defensive and the fear that somebody might appear suddenly who would pounce on me made me desperate. I had a fixed idea on my mind, the only idea, flee and save myself no matter how. Once in a while a breach opened among the bushes which allowed me to see the blue of the sea. I was nearing the shore and this was instinctively my objective, because my visual field there would be wider and I could learn of the position of my persecutors and besides I could run faster. More than logical reasoning it was instinct that guided me.

A small rock hill of steep slope marked the abrupt end of the woody area. On the other side, the sand of the virgin beach. At the sudden apparition of the rocks before my sight I did not have time to stop and I collided against them, my body laid almost at a slant against the sharp and cutting stones. I rapidly drew away from the rocks and started to climb them to span the obstacle and reach the white sand. My whole body, black as patent leather, was covered in blood and sweat, the soles of my bare feet stung, my hands hurt from the many scratches they bore. My nakedness facilitated my movements as I grabbed on to the stones with one hand to climb the hill, because in the other one I carried a long lance tipped by a very polished, sharp and pointed white stone.

I reached the top of the rocks and I was ready to jump the few yards that separated me from the very white sands of the wide and deserted beach. I was starting to hear noises behind me made by the group of persecutors who were getting closer, I clearly heard the crunch of the branches breaking in their path and the murmur of voices mixed in a din of savage howls.

I jumped and something new happened. In the air, before the momentum I had gathered allowed me to touch the ground, I felt separated to one side while I saw how the man dropped to the floor in his desperate flight.

That sturdy black man of medium height and wild appearance who had dropped to the sand and stayed on the ground for a moment squatting like a monkey, in spite of his obviously exhaustion managed now to stand up with unbelievable dexterity and was swiftly running the length of the beach in a direction parallel to the sea. His body glistened in the sun and he looked like a black ebony figure moving on the sands of the beach. In his hand was his lance as his only weapon. His attire was almost nothing. For an only garment he wore a loin cloth apparently made of leaves. From his ears hung two hoops so large that they almost brushed on his shoulders. His nose had been pierced with a big hole in its center where he wore another similar ring of smaller size.

From his neck hung several necklaces made from seeds and shells, and he also displayed strings of seeds around his ankles.

His appearance was that of a man who, despite his primitive state, did not seem to be aggressive or dangerous. He seemed like that type of savage man who lives from fishing and hunting. He ran without looking back. I again saw myself hurrying along the sand, playing the role of that life, after having watched myself in the figure of the savage black man from outside.

I turned and looked for an instant. Through the very spot where I had jumped a large group of men as black as I but with different appearance burst our into the clearing in the sand. I sped up my run and headed for the seashores where the waves broke against a huge hill or rocks which I would try to climb its top into the water. I was the only way to safety.

I reached the high hill and started the difficult climb. It was a very tall rock and it was hard to hold on to it because the protrusions on its surface were few, but in spite of it my urgency to save my life and the fear of being overcome gave me energy to go on.

I had climbed a few yards when the others reached the lower edge of the rocks. They threw rocks and lances which miraculously did not hit me. Their threatening gestures charged with anger and hate told more than words. They started to climb after me.

These men had an appearance very different from mine. They wore more abundant attire. They wore on their foreheads around their heads something similar to colored ribbons trimmed with short feathers of various colors. They wore necklaces, armbands and bracelets of vivid colors on their wrists and ankles. Their faces and chests were decorated with signs in various colors. Small skirts made of dry straw cinched their waists.

I was already reaching the top. I felt stimulated because I knew I would be safe. My movements became slow due to the fatigue, and the pain on my skin from the scratches sustained in my run and the wounds the cutting rocks has given my hands. The ache in my feet was sharp. I was almost about to reach the cusp.

Suddenly a strong hand, like a claw, seized my ankle. I tried to get loose, but couldn't because others were already grabbing my other foot and they pulled with animal force. In spite of everything I could fight and go on climbing. I was already on the top after having resisted the animal force that was pulling down on me, but surrounded by part of the group that persecuted me. Already on my feet, each one pushed me to the other in a macabre game of triumph, a prelude to what would follow, fed by hate and the most savage mockery ever before imagined, beyond all reason. We looked like a horde of savage animals.

My instincts prevailed above all feeling of hate, fear or desperation. A superhuman effort to get loose from that infernal circle and jump into the emptiness was my last intent to free myself from the savage tribe. I thud my arms out with all my strength and pushed two of the men, who fell off the cliff. I still remember the sound of the impact of their bodies against the rocks. A hand rose holding a long pole with a sharp point. I tried to dodge it, but its outline got lost in the sunlight ahead that blinded me and seemed to give its last flash of life. The sharp pole pierced my chest going through my body.

I again saw myself separated from the scenery as a spectator or my own act. The images started to dissipate in a whitish fog, while I watched terrified the last moment when that pile of beasts adorned with beautiful colors tore their victim's body into pieces and began to devour him.

The world, silent at times, in which I was protagonist and spectator at the same time of the last moments of some of my former incarnations, in which I experienced and appreciated my own deaths as a distant recollection erased from my spiritual memory which I again relived, constituted a moving tremendously impressive spectacle which will never be erased from my mind.

A PREVIEW OF WHAT WILL HAPPEN?

The infinite space of fog which surrounded me kept in me the sensation of total quiet, where the emotional states remained unalterable. I did not experience anything, all feeling disappeared. I did not perceive absolutely anything around me other than the deep fog which at the same time generated a very white faint light, hard to detail.

The unknown presence that I sensed from the tensest moments in my new dimension made itself felt with more intensity.

Another new and sudden change took place in a new mixture of strange sensations that filled me. I had the impression that my figure grew at the same time that the light that surrounded me was becoming more intense and like a large white ball little by little drew further away from me. I was floating in a vacuum in the midst of the dark space, as if the huge ball of light and my being were the center of everything, all that existed in it. I saw the twinkling sparks in every direction of stars of different sizes and intensities, some varying in shades between white and yellow, some bluish and others reddish. All those stars seemed to throb in the immense vault of the infinite universe. The darkness was absolute as in the black tunnel through which I ascended to the light.

-I will show you what will happen-, said a voice, which I immediately recognized. It was that of the elderly man who had been closest to me during my stay in the light and who accompanied me when leaving it. On this opportunity I did not hear it as before, but it seemed to resound like an echo in the whole space that surrounded me and came from all directions. When perceiving its sonority I noticed that its echo repeated itself disappearing in the distance, as if the words had been spoken in a large area surrounded by high mountains on the slopes of which it multiplied with abundance of tremendously impressive repetitions, like thundering in space.

Perhaps all that I tell next may be the most significant part of my postmortem experience, for its relevance, rarity and the shocking effect which it cause and still causes in me when I meditate about it all and which I have been able to understand clearly, what process most difficult for me to explain.

The great ball of light which had ceased to envelope me and moved away located itself exactly before me and grew like a large, circular, perfectly flat movie screen, and started to come closer, to such a point that it seemed I could touch it just by extending my arms ahead. From its borders, which seemed very distant to me, it started to change color and slowly turned into very dark blue, almost black. In its center appeared an enormous sky blue ball sprinkled with immense quite stains. A rapid effect of closeness was again produced and I felt myself floating in the space in which the great blue and white ball was suspended.

The white stains that covered a section of the blue on the great ball drew aside and the continents appeared before me with perfect definition, with their intense greenery, surrounded by the beautiful blue of the seas, separated from each other by an irregular white line drawn by the waves of the coasts. It was a fascinating spectacle and so beautiful that what I experienced on watching it could not be exactly described with words.

The solid, liquid and gaseous zones of the Earth showed themselves to my eyes clearly defined. This time, contrary from my previous visions, so to call them, I could perceive noises and experience different feelings; every type of feeling pervaded me in a strange mixture of emotions.

A strange premonition overcome me and the unknown of what would be that I was about to see troubled me, after having heard the elderly man's voice announcing that I would see what was going to happen. Was something going to happen to me immediately? What was going to happen and when? I felt a little fear.

The North American continent appeared first. The voice again reached me. I heard it clearly saying, "This will happen at the end of these years."

I saw how horrible earthquakes broke out along the area near the West coast of the United States. Fire and lava gushed from the entrails of the earth and an enormous gap opened swallowing whole cities. The ground pulled away from the continent forming a narrow and long island to the West of the solid portion, separated by a narrow strip of sea. Getting closer allowed me almost to participate in scenes that took place everything; men killed each other in vandalic acts and street brawls. Important figures died in assassinations. I sensed, through a natural knowledge like a telepathic message of wisdom, that the North America nation disintegrated and one state of the Union separated after a long conflict. I cannot pinpoint which one it is, but it is located in the Southwest near or on the border with Mexico. I cannot exactly define the places and the positions because I did not distinguish the frontiers.

After this a large explosion followed like a potent atomic bomb which accidentally caused great disasters in the whole territory and extended to the liquid zones of the planet. In the peninsula of Florida great disasters took place which I cannot define as natural or caused by the hand of man. It was how the peninsula split in two and became separated from the continent by a wide strip of sea which ran East to West.

As if in a movie the shape of North America faded out and the area of Central America and the West Indies faded in, where due to the disasters suffered in Florida, huge waves which went around the world caused horrible tidal waves on the coasts of the Gulf of Mexico and the West Indies. A strong earthquake destroyed a large part of the eastern surface of the island of Cuba.

The South American continent appeared, where just as on the West coast of North America violent and disastrous seismic movements took place which caused great calamities in an area located around the zone of Peru, Ecuador and northern Chile. At the same time cruel civil wars were fought in that area. When I fixed my attention on the South cone of the continent, the voice was heard again.

-What you see will start at the beginning of the years.

When I heard this assertion, something was not made quite clear in my mind, because when the voice referred to the end of the years or the beginning of these, I do not understand whether he was referring to the beginning of the next century or the end of the present one, or to eras that I cannot imagine. I have not yet understood these revelations.

Little by little, in a process that seemed to me replayed in slow motion, I saw how the appearance in this zone changed from its green vegetation to a yellowish shade, the fields turned arid and extremely hot as if the sun burned and destroyed all animal and vegetal life in this area. It finally turned almost into a desert.

Like a giant poster stuck to a huge wall, the continents continued appearing which like hieroglyphics transmitted to me with great clarity the events that were taking place, crossing the barrier of times and distances in the future history.

The images again faded out and I made out the European continent. As if the disaster of the earthquakes and volcanic eruptions were an epidemic spread throughout the surface of the globe, I again saw that in the Italian peninsula huge craters opened, seas of burning fire-red lava spread over the Northern lands and horrible earthquakes destroyed everything, sowing death and desolation in huge areas.

In Great Britain an event took place similar to that seen in the North American continent. A gigantic and potent explosion occurred which reminds me of the movie images taken in World War I. Enormous smoke mushroom rose high in the sky. I saw the destruction of a large and important city, perhaps London, sowing death all over, as if a very powerful bomb with great destructive capability had been dropped over that city.

The area of the Mediterranean Sea next rose to my eyes giving way the African continent. I saw that a great desert on the north, which I suppose must be the Sahara; in a long a slow process grew in every direction. And in the South cone of this continent the same repeated itself which I had observed on the south of South America. The sunlight turned reddish, and like a slow and invisible fire it slowly turned the whole area into an almost desert zone in which flora and fauna, everything living, died.

-Everything you are seeing will continue happening for the last years-, the elderly man's voice announced, like an echo coming from infinity.

The large continent of Asia was displayed, sprinkled in the South with gleaming white points that I suppose were the snowy caps of the high elevations. In the northeast the same seismic catastrophes repeated themselves in which volcanic eruptions, avalanches of burning lava, earthquakes, fissures in the earth surface mixed. The large islands of the Japanese archipelago split in pieces and were separated by the sea, other smaller ones disappeared in the depths of the ocean. In this catastrophe I noticed bigger damages and calamities that in the former manifestations of disasters observed elsewhere. There disasters in island zones caused huge waves which spread all over the sea and the water entered the solid zones razing everything in its path.

I was finally before Australia, where, for the third time, the strange phenomenon reproduced which I could not understand in the beginning, in which the solar light produced a malignant, destructive effect on everything living, gradually erasing every vestige of life and greenery over a large part of the solid surface, turning the fields in the South into arid, dusty and deserted zones.

Each and every one of the events presented itself as if in a colored dream. The images of the continents finally moved away which had separately paraded before my eyes like giant maps full of realities. I saw the whole surface of the planet displayed on a single plane and the continents lost their outlines dissipating like in a waving fog, moving to the background. I then clearly saw the image of a face in the foreground, but with a certain translucence which allowed seeing the wavy motion of the background, as if foreboding something that would affect the whole planet. A strange symbol.

It was the face of a man, dark, with a long face, very fine features, slightly Roman nose, a short beard, very dark hair, as were his perfectly well drawn eyebrows, and the hair trimmed just above his shoulders. Although his expression was discretely serene, somewhat sweet, his black and large eyes with a profound look had a certain diabolic spark which on observing them caused a certain unrest in me. A man who looked by his appearance from Arabic origins, dressed in a black robe in the style characteristic of them. When my attention was fixed on this image, the elderly man's voice let itself be heard in an imperative and energetic tone.

-This man will be known by everyone at the end of the years. He will be the opposite of the Messiah and will have much power.

Following, after the image of this man dissolved into thin air like smoke, a new picture appeared, always maintaining the initial translucence and the background. I saw the solemn parade of a big funeral in which large crowds and very important figures took part, headed by a large carriage behind which rows of men who looked like Catholic cardinals by the clothes they wore walked in rows leading the crowd. They walked slowly rocking the red color capes in rhythm with their footsteps. In the rear part of the open carriage was a coffin with a glass cover, inside which an elderly man's body could be seen, also dressed in red, whose face I could not make out.

-The next one will be the last, –The elderly man's voice once again said in a solemn tone -and what happens will take place in the last years.

I remained with the feeling of immovability in which a marble statue could be, with coldness, with no feeling that would alter my emotional state, like someone who has been hypnotized and forced to see all that he must.

-These that you see, -the voice of that one whom I could not see but I knew was there somewhere went on saying-, will live together with men the last times.

He had not concluded his words when the last image appeared before me. Groups of being presented themselves, very similar to the ones I has seen in the last instant before parting from the light. Dwarfish figures, whose almost transparent and colorless clothes gave the impression of being, with very thin bodies, shaved head disproportionally large in comparison with their skinny and minute bodies, big and slanted eyes and large ears. This last rose like a flash of lightning which put an end to the parade of events and figures.

All that I perceived instantly disappeared and I remained forming part of nothingness. That strange state of conscience which had like a silent beating made me feel strangely alive slowly weakened. I could only hear a heavy breathing which came from all directions as if an enormous giant slept an eternal and deep sleep taking up all the space that surrounded me, making me feel tremendously minuscule.

RETURN TO MY BODY

I heard a constant murmur of voices from very fat off, very remote, so distant that they barely reached me as a whisper. In my semi consciousness I tried to decipher and understand what voices and who spoke, to what the agitation was due that excited them, for it seemed to me for a moment that they argued.

I thought of myself. I felt imprisoned, so harshly confined in a space in which it seemed to me body did not fit. This was a very brief instant. I wanted to free myself of those invisible ties that immobilized and did not let me even breath. I suddenly managed it. I breathed deeply, very deeply, as much so as I believed to ever have, with such intensity that I felt how my chest enlarged as my lungs swelled with air.

-Doctor, doctor, he's alive! –A woman yelled.

Her voice stood out clearly amid the murmur of voices that I heard from afar.

I tried to open my eyes, but found it impossible to do. I felt an enormous weight as if my eyelids were lead. In that brief instant a second of consciousness allowed me to realize I felt a severe headache that was stronger near the nape, a constant and terribly sharp pain. I felt strong hands grab my legs, while others grabbed both my arms and raised me from the hard and cold surface on which I lay, so cold that I felt it through my clothes. Another hand held up my head. I could not move, I lacked the strength. I felt myself being lifted and in a moment they laid me, gently, on a cushioned surface. It seemed the dream or the nightmare would not end. First the shadows, then the light and later the terrible physical discomfort. If someone has described hell, I think this closely resembled its characteristics. I later heard a man's unfamiliar voice.

-Lay him down carefully. –He said with authority.

I later heard a mixture of noises of engines and sirens which slowly grew further away until I again fell asleep. I did not know how long I remained in that state, although it seemed to me a very long time. Some subsequent details make me suppose it was much shorter.

BACK TO REALITY

I woke up in the instant I felt a thin and smooth object pulled from under my tongue. At my side, by the bed on which I lay, was standing a woman in a white uniform. She was very tall, or at least that is how she seemed to me watching her from below on my bed. Chubby, with slow and deliberate gestures, as if each movement had been studied, giving signs of knowing her occupations well, she looked with her bulging eyes, like those of a frog, at the thermometer she held in her hand. Then she turned to me, her cold and indifferent look suddenly turning to an expression of surprise at seeing I was watching her.

-Well, the man finally woke up! You're hard to peel. Quite a scare you gave to the ambulance men who brought you. –She said with the casualness of someone who comments on a baseball game with a friend.

I suddenly remembered what had happened in the street, the sharp blow on my head, the two men, the strange dream I thought I had dreamt. To my mind came the marvels, the wonderful wellbeing and happiness I enjoyed amidst that light. Finding myself there I felt sad and disappointed.

-But, why was I awakened, when I felt so good? –I asked disillusioned.

-Why, did you expect to go on sleeping for all eternity? –The nurse asked jokingly, which I did not find at all funny. She noticed it. I would have liked to answer her "Yes", but it wasn't worth it.

I tried to sit up, but severe dizziness stopped me and at the same time I felt a sharp pain in the back of my head. I could raise my arm and feel with my hand, but I had a thick bandage around my forehead. I was obviously wide awake, very alive.

A long time elapsed; nobody else had come to my bed. I was anxious to know what information there was on what exactly was going on with me. Finally another nurse came into the room with a small tray in her hands which she placed on the small metal table by the head of my bed.

While she did this, I ran my eyes for the first time over the room where I was, to which I had not paid attention before, being absorbed in my thoughts. The furniture was made up of two beds, two small tables and two metal armchairs. The next bed, to my right, was empty.

This new nurse, shorter than the other one, slender, smiling, with pleasant mannerisms, made me feel more relaxed and at ease as to address her. Right after she greeted me with her spontaneous smile and her friendly gestures, I felt encouraged and trusting. This was the opportunity I used to ask her questions about what had happened with me, how I had arrive there, in what condition, what my state was when I arrived at the hospital.

Engulfed in an avalanche of questions, she proceeded to clam all my uneasiness, informing me that someone had called the hospital where I was on the telephone, reporting an accident and saying that several persons had assaulted another who seemed to be dead on the street. The call had been made at 11:15. An ambulance was immediately sent. She told me that at the very moment in which the doctor who examined me when they found me on the pavement, after having made every effort possible trying to resuscitate me, all resources exhausted, already giving up, had considered me dead and was ready to leave, a female assistant noticed I had suddenly breathed and told him I was alive. According to what those who accompanied him commented, he was amazed at what had happened when he verified that my heart was again beating.

-What time did I arrive at the hospital?

-You went into the ward at eleven thirty-five, unconscious. –Was the nurse's reply-. It had taken twenty minutes.

She went on to say that I had received a sharp blow to the back of my head, which had not caused a fracture, but that I had suffered, due to it, a strong contusion, from which I had recovered miraculously and incredibly fast. That I had a wound in the back of the head where I suffered the blow and it had been sutured.

I looked though the frame of the open door I had in front of my bed to the wall of the outer hall which was in front of the room, where a white clock with large black numbers told 6:10 in the morning. Seven hours had passed.

After having made me swallows several tablets and giving me a shot, the nurse left the room.

Hardly a yard away from my bed, on the side wall, a wide open large glass window let in the light and the cool air of the morning that was beginning. Through it I could see a patch of the sky. My eyes fixed on the celestial blue; I remembered minutely all that I thought I had dreamed, detail by detail.

Something in my subconscious told me it had not been a dream, more so upon remembering the first moment in which I had seen myself separated from my body and on thinking of the way in which I had recovered consciousness in the first lucid moment, adding to it what the nurse had recounted who stated that they gave me for dead for a moment.

The morning got light. The clean and blue sky was a hymn to life. The light of the rising sun that come in through the window warmed my feet through the sheet that covered me.

The song of a bird reached my ears from outside as a gift, announcing the awaking of a new day, a new sunrise, a new life.

NEW CONCEPTS

Every day, for a long time, I have meditated about everything that I learned by this experience, a moment from which my life totally changed at having acquired the conviction, by experience, that beyond our present life in this third dimension, there is a better one.

When I think about the first moment when I saw myself separated from my body, just dead and not having yet become convinced of it, when I saw myself lying on the floor and I watched other live persons, I understand that all those who separate from the matter continue and indefinite existence and are totally liberated, not only to have the capacity wholly to understand the great sense of death and true life to enrich themselves in their new dimension with all the knowledge and the experience acquired in their last incarnated physical existence, but also through the experiences of other lives – independently from the degree of social or intellectual development reached in each one of them,- which will remain stored in their astral memory, that it to say, in their liberate vital energy.

The souls or the vital energy, or however you may wish to call them, will possess unlimited capabilities as far as acquiring knowledge in general, since their transit through different lives allows them to accumulate an enormous whole variety of material as well spiritual teaching which constitute and immense source of wisdom and understanding of natural, pure and essential knowledge of all that exist, in the concept of life in our and other worlds on the physical as well as the energetic plane.

Through a process of natural progression in which the interrelation between what is spiritual and material balances as on a scale, we go on evolving in our life, in a state of conscience which results in the wellbeing that we experience daily in our existence, which depends on the general behavior and attitude which we maintain through it. Depending on the degree of cleanliness in which our conscience may be, we will live in peace with ourselves and with others, and also as a part of human society in general, and the enjoyment or not of the other plane of existence will depend on state of conscience. On that spiritual plane we acquire, to sum it up, a state of plenitude in dependency on everything positive assimilated in each one of our former lives, since once definitely liberated from matter and our memory being left unblocked, we enjoy full capacity to enrich our intellect based on the learning of the material and spiritual existence, because we are constant energetic forces temporarily carrying physical bodies and vice versa, since matter transforms, but it is invariable and indestructible.

Due to my experience, I think that on the invisible plane where we all go once we separate from our physical bodies, not only the vital energies of human beings are transferred but everything that exists in the plane of the third dimension and even inhabitants and beings from other worlds and civilizations which unarguably form a part of our material universe. For that reason I ask myself, Might it possible that being free from matter we may reincarnate in creatures of other worlds? Might we store in our astral mind remembrances of material existences from other worlds?

We as spiritual beings who temporarily inhabit a physical body issue constant energetic fluids which extend in all directions and the purity and positive or negative intensity, source of life which saturates each material thing that surrounds us, will depend on the measure in which our passions and feeling may project. Our dwellings, the places where we walk, the places we frequently attend little by little become impregnated with that energy, not only that arising from one individual, but that of thousands and even millions, which causes us to leave a trail, a print of our transit through the material world which could perhaps affect the lives of many people.

Many have told me, -and it has even happened to me-, that they have been in a place for a length of time and they have felt restless, uncomfortable and have even experienced physical discomfort; others, on the contrary, have enjoyed full physical and spiritual comfort. All this that we experience is very often caused by the positivism and negativism of the energies accumulated in the matter that surrounds us, deriving from energetic emanations from other individuals who were before, generally for a long time, in the place we visit or where we may be permanently, persons who left their trail and who may be alive or perhaps dead.

In each life experience incarnated or separate from matter, the being has free will to follow his behavior in a positive or negative way, but this will be influenced by the medium that surrounds him. In many cases the spirit does not progress, on the contrary, it becomes stagnant, regresses or remains in a state unconsciousness with respect to the difference existing between right and wrong. When this state remains in the being and the negative forces prevail, it is very difficult or impossible for the energetic being, once liberate from the physical body, to be able to cross the dark frontiers and gloomy antechamber to the light, so it will remain as a part of it, a product of the harmony that exist between both and their common characteristics. Only a positive spirit or one which stays in a progressive state toward positivism could reach the light.

Having full certainty of the existence of another life, be it acquired through experience, by faith, through studies or by conviction, we should prepare ourselves for it in the course of the present one, no matter in which way, but always watching that our behavior, our actions and our projection in general be positive, acting in good faith, with honesty and love to ourselves as well as to others, because in the measure in which our energies, impelled by well-intentioned thoughts, feeling and emotions, may gradually transform us all the time into more positive beings, in the measure in which we may offer this positivism, we will pave the road to cross the dark and terrible frontier which many cannot clear, through which we must unavoidably travel on our way to the light.

Depending on the positive force that we may carry in our spiritual being the possibility will exist of reaching the permanent and undying light in order to enjoy its benefit and form a part of it, a light in which everything that exists in the physical universe inhabits in perfect energetic replica, a light from which we will come out to reincarnate and to which we will again return in a continuous cycle of depuration and improvement until the ultimate moment in which we will form an integral and inseparable part of it fused in one single unit.

Harmonious love and peace are the bases which constitute all that is good that our spiritual being holds from our physical birth and we should, from a very early stage, for the good of ourselves, of everyone and of all, maintain it and enrich it with that essence.

Love, peace and wisdom constitute the energies which integrate our spiritual being when we finally reach the plane of light. Conscience, memory and intelligence are spirit and when love is added to this it is apt to form a part of the light, because it is light. Love and peace integrate the world of light in all its plenitude in the other life, a plane where true and full happiness exists.

WHAT ARE WE?

The memories of my experience constantly return to my mind and each moment I discover something new. I think about all the wealth of new acquired knowledge, of the new bases to think about what man is as human kind and about the immense universe of riches that make up the individual in his unit of material and spiritual being, of the visible and invisible space of which he forms and essential part, and I dare affirm that being is undying and perfectly conditioned to travel through unlimited enrichment and enlargement processes which take it to an exalted state of progressive perfection in the incarnations as well as in spirituality, like an exceptional entity within the immense variety of genera existing in the universe, on the physical plane as well as on that of liberated energetic force, which is one of its alternate stages of continuity of progress.

The mater that makes up the whole visible universe to which we belong does not perish, but, through a long repetitive process of birth, development and death, transforms, liberating its energy. A tree upon drying transforms into organic matter, as happens with animals and everything physically alive. Energy once liberates passes in perfect replica to another plane continuing life.

We know that the human body and every living body, including mater which we call dead, generate energy. This has different intensities in each physical body, which varies depending on the different states of excitement to which matter is directly or indirectly subjected, just as the intensity of its emanations and projection also varies.

The liberated vital energy or spirit may be visible at some time by specific persons. This is because, once this is liberated, it can move and transfer itself at its free will and travel through where it did when it occupied a physical body. I even dare affirm that thanks to this self-determination, the energetic being could select the new body in which it wishes to reincarnate at the birth of a new infant to live a next existence, be it from infinity, by simple wish or from experimental necessity.

Many persons have established communication with those who have already separated from matter and who are still indirectly tied to live beings, perhaps due to pending affairs left without resolving. And in the same telepathic way in which two astral bodies can communicate between themselves they can do so with living persons, through special natural gifts of extrasensory perception which these latter have and which allow them to carry out such a communication, who on their part have the capability to contact with these spiritual entities. The intention of establishing this type of communication can originate from either part. These communications are very revealers of secrets, transmitters of messages and even enriches of knowledge for the physical individual, as well as for the ethereal being, since the later, besides, can and has the capacity to assimilate knowledge proceeding from the physical plane.

The value, the determination, the geniality or the aptitude in different activities of an individual's life very often has an origin beyond that arising from conjectures and mental analyses, but rather they are intentional foreign intelligent emanations, directed to him by a spiritual being. Many individual perform acts and even make statements in their lives that are exceptional and beyond what is common in a regular and normal being. However, in these cases this can be induced by a non-physical being who directed energetic impulses through telepathic to the vital energy imprisoned in the individual's physical body and it thus passes to his conscience. The individual unconsciously acts or manifests himself as if moved by his own intuition or reasoning. Many persons, after having performed some particular act, ask themselves who it was possible for them to have done or said such a thing. Generally when these cases occur, the individual presents a heightened state of lucidity and clear judgment outside what is normal, beyond his apparent capacity of intellect.

The individual energetic force is an indivisible part of nature in its continual evolution. This force keeps accumulation of incalculable universal emotions, knowledge and memories. Although in the physical being the memory is contained in the neuronal energy of the brain, another immense wealth of knowledge exists that is stored in its astral memory, which does not have access to its conscious memory in the physical state. This has been proven in experiments carried out through hypnosis in which some persons have been transported to several former incarnations and it has been possible to observe stages of their other experiences when unblocking their neuronal memory and entering the spiritual one.

In my case, I have not been one to remember dreams, so I have generally said that I don't dream, as my sleep has always been deep and pleasant; however, I have on numbered occasions recalled dreams where I have seen myself in circumstances little known and uncommon to my life, playing out scenes where I have been another person, which I considered a product of my imagination. After my experience, however, I think the opposite. I am sure that being asleep one can, in specific moments, remember passages from former lives which are stored in our vital energetic memory.

The halos of light that surrounded the heads and bodies of those whom I encountered in my death, in the light, can also sometimes be seen around physical bodies.

I remember that, years ago, something happened to me in that regard which caught my attention greatly, but I could not at that moment find an explanation for it. I was in the audience at the performance of a stage play. The playhouse was dark and the only lights there were the ones on the stage. A woman in front of me did not allow me to see certain sections of the stage. I moved constantly in my seat from one side to the other. There was a moment when I noticed, and I continued seeing it during the whole performance, that there was a slightly phosphorescent faint white light around the lady's head and at the moments when the stage turned dark, that light became brighter and more visible to my eyes.

There is much to meditate, analyze and discuss about this subject, and all that I could describe and explain around what I tell in the present text would be unending, but there is something of which there is no doubt, that all this evolution in the animal and vegetable life, as well as the growth, development and progress of the energetic being and that unending cycle of physical death, birth, disembodiment and reincarnation have an origin that can only be created, ordered, controlled and directed by a far superior non-material intelligent Entity which nobody has been able to reach, which neither living nor dead have been able to decipher and those who may have known It have never been able to describe It, Something superior and unreachable which exercises total power over all things visible and invisible, a supreme Something which is everything, which comes from everywhere and goes everywhere, which is always present and makes Itself wisely and subtly felt in the course of the existences in their different states, dimensions and planes, an Entity that overcomes the plane of light I knew.

The mysteries that surround the true and undying spiritual life being whatever they might be, we cannot deny its existence and its truth, imagined by some, divined by others, described by certain persons gifted with special faculties, acclaimed by every religion from different points of view and under different concepts, and invisible world for the "living", but real by nature, the world where the "dead" live, a world I knew and from which I had the opportunity to return to be able to offer you this brief testimony of my death.

THE END

INDEX

Page

www.ingramcontent.com/pod-product-compliance
Lightning Source LLC
Chambersburg PA
CBHW060643130626

46555CB00002B/941